SWEET DREAMS

★ A Lift-the-Flap Bedtime Story ★

Sue Porter

DK

I used to sleep in a little crib.

Now I sleep in my big new room in my big
new bed, with Tiddle, my teddy.

Before we go to sleep, we look
at the shadows under the bed.

There are shadows up near the ceiling, too. Raggy and Wallop like to sleep there. They are not scared.

Sometimes everybody gets together in my big new bed.

But usually it's just Tiddle and me.

We pretend to be
little birds in our nest,

or little bats
sleeping upside down.

We peek out of holes
like little worms,

or little kangaroos
in pockets.

Dad reads us a story and says good night.
Then he says, "Close your eyes everybody. I'll
put sweet dreams in with a kiss on your eyelids."

"Now keep them shut. Don't let the dreams escape!"

Everybody has sweet dreams.

Tig and Mary
dream they are...

Wallop...

Scruffy...

Then I dream about the shadows. And in the
shadows there is a monster. It frightens me.
It wakes me up. I hide under the covers.
I keep very still. I keep very quiet.
It is very hot.

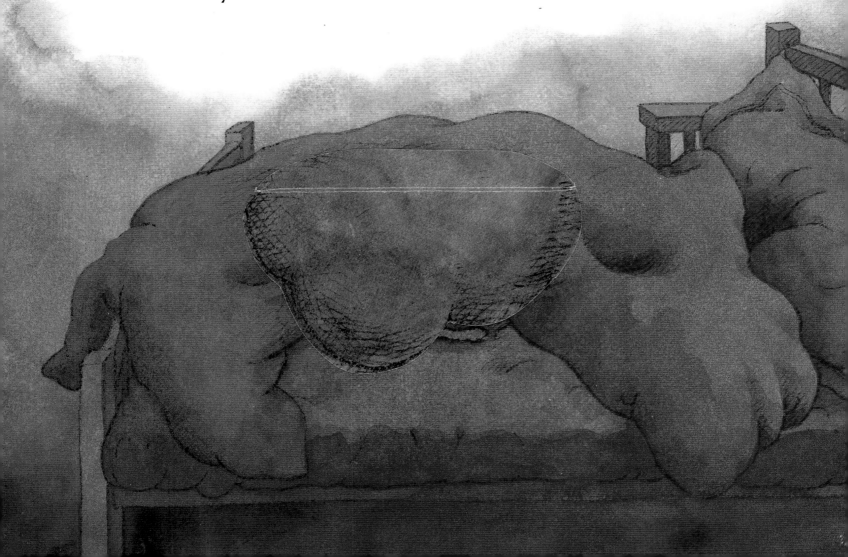

Then Tiddle whispers in my ear.
Tiddle knows what to do.
"Stick out your tongue!
Wiggle your fingers! Shout –

'Hey...

We turn on the light and look
under the bed.

And I can hear Mom and Dad
downstairs in the kitchen.

The next night I tell Dad about the monster in the shadows. He says, "Do you want to leave the light on tonight?"
"No," I say. "I'm not scared."

When we are in bed, Dad kisses in
sweet dreams. This time we don't peek.

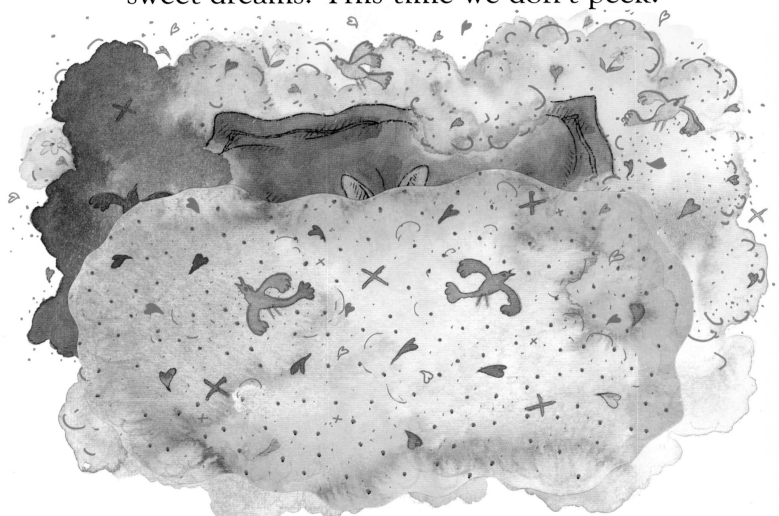

And then we have the very best dreams
of all.

We sing songs in the trees with pink parrots...
and dance on the tops of tall towers.